THE
CLASS ELECTION
FROM THE
BLACK LAGOON

THE
CLASS ELECTION
FROM THE
BLACK LAGOON

by Mike Thaler
Illustrated by Jared Lee

SCHOLASTIC INC.

New York   Toronto   London   Auckland   Sydney
Mexico City   New Delhi   Hong Kong   Buenos Aires

To Dennis Adler, who makes *Heaven and Mirth* real—M.T.
A salute to all the men and women in our armed forces —J.L.

Visit us at www.abdopublishing.com Reinforced library bound edition published
in 2011 by Spotlight, a division of ABDO Publishing Group, 8000 West 78th Street,
Edina, Minnesota 55439. This edition was reprinted by permission of Scholastic Inc.
No part of this publication may be reprinted in whole or in part, or in any form or by
any means, electronic or mechanical, without written permission of the publisher.
For information regarding permission, write to Scholastic Inc., Attention: Permissions
Department, 557 Broadway, New York, NY 10012.

Printed in the United States of America, Melrose Park, Illinois.
082010
012011

 This book contains at least 10% recycled materials.

Library of Congress Cataloging-in-Publication Data
This title was previously cataloged with the following information:
Thaler, Mike, 1936-,
  The class election from the black lagoon / by Mike Thaler ; pictures by Jared Lee.
     p. cm. – (Black lagoon adventures ; #3)
  Summary: Everyone has to run for an office in Mrs. Green's class election.
  [1. Elections–Fiction. 2. Schools-Fiction] I. Lee, Jared D., ill. II. Title.
  PZ7.T3 Cl 2003
  [E]–dc22   2004272632

ISBN: 978-1-59961-810-4 (reinforced library bound edition)

All Spotlight books have reinforced library binding and are
manufactured in the United States of America.

CONTENTS

CHAPTER 1
ELECTION FEVER

We're having a class election. Mrs. Green says everyone has to run for something. I'd like to run for the hills. Maybe I can just let my nose run.

I don't want to be vice president because all they do is give advice. And I don't want to be secretary. You just spend hours keeping minutes.

And I don't want to be treasurer—I'm not so good at math.

I guess I'll run for president. Maybe they'll put my face on Mount Rushmore or on a three-dollar bill.

CHAPTER 2
CANDIED-DATES

Mrs. Green says we'll vote in two weeks and that we have to campaign and give speeches. This is going to be a cam*paign* in the neck. We may even have a debate.

Uh-oh, Doris is running against me. She says she wants to be the first woman president ever. That would make *me* the first loser ever.

Penny is going to be her campaign manager. Eric says that he'll be mine because he'd hate to see me lose to a girl.

Freddy wants to be *vice* president because the *vise* is his favorite tool in woodshop. Derek wants to be secretary because it has "s-e-c-r-e-t" in it. And Randy is running for treasurer because he thinks he'll get to keep all the money.

This is going to be a tough election.

HUBIE'S A BIG LOSER. VOTE FOR DORIS.

11

CHAPTER 3
A FAST SLOGAN

Eric says that we need a campaign slogan.

"What about—*Vote for me*?" I say.

"Not enough pizzazz," says Eric.

I scratch my head.

"What about—*I'm a resident, make me president*?" I ask.

"Better," says Eric.

"Whoa, I think I have it. What about—*Don't be a booby, vote for Hubie*?!" I shout.

"Bingo!" cheers Eric.

13

"Now we need some posters. Doris already has some up in the hall," Eric adds.

"What's her slogan?" I ask.

"It's time for a change," Eric smiles.

"Sounds like a diaper ad," I laugh.

CHAPTER 4

OFF THE WALL

I'm not a great artist, but I can draw good dinosaurs. So I draw a T-Rex on five posters and print out my slogan.

Then Eric and I tape them up in the hall—next to Doris's posters. Doris even has one up in the boys' bathroom. Now, that's dirty politics. Someone's a traitor.

So I sneak into the girls' bathroom and put up a poster. Great causes take great risks. If I get caught, it could ruin my political career.

I can see it now. I am running for President of the United States. I'm ahead in the polls.

Then the story of how I snuck into the girls' bathroom is leaked. I'm all washed up in politics. My campaign stalls. My career goes down the drain. I'll never be flushed with victory.

Hey, their bathroom looks just like ours—what's the big deal?

CHAPTER 5
PRESIDENTS' PRECEDENCE

I go to the library, and Mrs. Beamster shows me a book about past presidents. There were lots of them and they were *all* famous.

The first was George Washington, D.C. He never told a lie because he had wooden teeth. He couldn't lie through his teeth. That's why a bridge is named after him.

YOU HAVE A NICE SMILE.

PRESIDENTS

THE
WHITE
HOUSE

ABE
L.

19

Then there was Abraham Lincoln. He didn't lie, either. Mrs. Beamster says that he walked ten miles just to return an overdue book. He lived in Gettysburg because they said he had a Gettysburg Address!

Then there was Teddy Roosevelt. He invented the teddy bear. I heard he belonged to a motorcycle gang called The Rough Riders. And they won the San Juan Hill climb.

Mrs. Beamster says that all the presidents were great men. And if I win the election, I'd be in good company. Yeah, but none of them had to run against girls!

CHAPTER 6
A PEACH OF A SPEECH

After school, Eric and I go to my house. It's time to write the speech. I'm inspired.

"My fellow students . . ." I begin.

"No good," says Eric. "You have to try and steal the girl vote."

"Dear girls and boys . . ." I start again.

"But you don't want to lose the boy vote," says Eric, folding his arms. He waits patiently.

I clear my throat and say, "Dear voters . . ."

"Good. Now, what's your platform?" asks Eric.

"I don't need a platform," I reply. "I'm tall enough."

"No, no, what do you stand for?" asks Eric.

I put my hand over my heart. "The national anthem," I reply.

Eric raises his arms and sighs.

GRRRR...

25

"No, no, what's your agenda?" Eric says impatiently.

"My gender's a boy," I laugh. Eric rolls his eyes.

"No, no, what will you do if you get elected?" He huffs and puffs.

"Be surprised," I smile.

CHAPTER 7
A SPECIAL DELIVERY

Well, I finally write my speech, but then I have to give it. I stand in front of the mirror and start, "Dear voters . . ."

"From the heart," says Eric.

"Deeeeer voters . . ." I sing.

"Good," smiles Eric. And he pats me on the back.

I puff out my chest, fold my arms, and cross my eyebrows.

"Deeeeer voters, I stand before you today, so I'll be tall enough. Tall enough to reach the high office of president—a president of the people, by the people, and for the people. A

president that will stand by you, sit by you, and walk by you—in the cafeteria, in the classroom, in the bathroom, on the playground, I'll be there. So next week—don't be a booby, vote for Hubie."

Eric gives me a standing ovation.

CHAPTER 8
DREAMS OF GLORY

I'm beginning to like this. What if I win?

What if I go on to become President of the United States?

I would go and live in the White House. Maybe I'll paint it green. Then it would be the Green House, and I could grow orchids. Then I'd have an *orchid-stra*.

I could do a lot of good for everybody. I would end global warming, war, and hunger. I would put a pizza place in every town and village. I would make recess longer and math class shorter.

I would outlaw spinach and
ban brussels sprouts. I would
make the U.S. Mint—the U.S.
Mint-chocolate chip. I would make
the weekend six days, and the
summer ten months. I would
change the eagle to a beagle and
make my dog the national symbol.

I would be famous. I'd have my own limousine, airplane, and skateboard. They would name things after me—Hubie Airport, Lake Hubie, and Hubieville.

I would go down in history . . . if I win.

UNITED STATAS

CHAPTER 9
THE BALLOT OF HUBIE COOL

But what if I *lose*? To a girl? To Doris? What a bummer!

I can see it now . . .

None of my friends would ever talk to me again.

No one would sit at my lunch table. I'd eat alone for the rest of my life. I couldn't ask anyone to pass the ketchup.

I wouldn't be popular—I'd be
poop-ular.

I'd be kicked off the baseball
team and have to turn in my little
league cap. I would have let
down every boy in school and
unborn generations of boys. I
couldn't join the Boy Scouts.

I'd better start campaigning . . .
now!

37

CHAPTER 10
A SHAKE-UP

"Now you have to go out, kiss babies, and shake hands," says Eric.

"Babies can't vote! There aren't even any in school," I answer.

"True, but there are lots of hands," smiles Eric.

Okay, so I go around and shake everybody's hand. I feel silly.

I shake Mrs. Green's claw and Coach Kong's paw. I shake, rattle, and roll.

DON'T BE A BOOBY VOTE FOR HUBIE

I even shake hands with
Fester Smudge. This can't be
very sanitary.

ZAP!

Then I go and have a milk shake.

41

CHAPTER 11
THE GREAT DEBATE

Well, Doris and I are in front of the whole class. I feel like I'm under a microscope. I should have combed my hair more, but Doris has a pimple on the end of her nose.

We shake hands and she goes first. She says that she's for women's rights and total equality. I ask her why she gets to go first.

"Because I'm a girl, of course," she sneers.

"Oh," I reply.

43

Then it's my turn. "Knock, knock!"

"Who's there?" says everyone.

"Debate," I answer.

"Debate who?!" shouts the class.

"Put debate on the hook and we'll go fishing!" I laugh.

"That's not funny," says Doris, poking me in the back.

"Is too," says I, poking her back.

"Is not," says Doris, stamping her foot.

"Is," I say, stamping mine.

"Not," says Doris, crossing her eyes.

"Is," says I, crossing mine.

We go on until the lunch bell rings and ends our debate.

CHAPTER 12
DORIS'S COOL MOVE

Unfair, unfair!

Doris says she's the candidate of the *Birthday Party*. She's buying ice cream bars for all the voters at lunch.

Everyone's lining up in drooling droves. My whole class. My best friends. Even Eric, my manager!

I'm betrayed in the cafeteria. I feel like that ancient Roman Emperor Julius Caesar Salad. Jabbed in the back with a dessert spoon. I feel *desserted*.

This is sweet-tooth politics. Underhanded. Underfooted. Underrated!

How can she stoop so low?

I better hurry before all the chocolate's gone!

CHAPTER 13

POLL POSITION

Yum, that was good. Now what can I do?

With my allowance, I couldn't afford to give out water. Anyway, I'm not going to buy votes. I'm going to stand on my principal. He may get angry, though.

I can't let Doris get ahead in the polls. The polls tell how people are planning to vote. I could climb the flag *poll*.

I could buy a horse and win the gallop *poll*. I could go to Antarctica and visit the South *Poll*. I could even go to *Poll*-land with a fishing *poll*.

How can I *poll* vault ahead? I have to do something to give Doris her just desserts.

I'M AHEAD.

CHAPTER 14
TAKING A STAND

I need to do something outstanding—something awesome, something that betters the school. But what?

I could mow the grass and have a lawn sale. I could rename the gym . . . Ted. I could take home plate home and put it in the dishwasher.

53

Wow! All the kids have dropped their ice cream wrappers on the floor. I'll pick them up. I'll be an environmental hero. I'll be the candidate of the *Mrs. Green Party*! I'll save the planet. This feels good.

Now I do stand for something.

PICK THOSE UP, HUBIE.

IT'S MY DUTY, MRS. GREEN.

CHAPTER 15
ELECTION JITTERS

The pre-election night is a rough one. What if no one votes for me? Not even the boys. What if I lose by a landslide?

The power of ice cream is awesome. If I vote for myself, at least I'll have one vote. But everyone will know whose it is. Eric got two ice cream bars. Even he may not vote for me.

When I fall asleep, I have a nightmare . . .

I'm climbing up a slippery giant ice cream sundae. It's a mountain of vanilla with hot fudge. Doris is sitting on top— laughing, with a cherry on her head. I keep slipping and sliding, and she keeps laughing louder and louder until finally there's a thunderous roar. And I'm covered in a vanilla landslide.

I wake up and my head's under my pillow. It's Election Day!

Z-Z-Z

57

CHAPTER 16
HIGH NOON

Mrs. Green passes out pieces of paper. I'm ready to pass out with nervousness. It's a secret ballot.

Doris looks very confident. She's got a box of doughnuts for

her victory party—chocolate-coconut. I really hope that everyone doesn't drop his or her napkins on the floor.

Well, I'm voting for me — doughnuts or not.

Mrs. Green collects the ballots. Our names are written on the chalkboard. Doris and I are on top. Mrs. Green marks one vote for Doris. I hope that's Doris's vote. Then she marks another vote for Doris. That's probably Freddy's. He can't resist chocolate-coconut.

Then she marks one vote for me. That's probably mine. I wonder if Doris will let me come to her victory party. Then she marks another vote for me!

GRRR.

VOTE

WINK.

Eric winks.

Wow! We're tied. It won't be a landslide after all. Mrs. Green marks another vote for me. And another. And another. I can't believe it!

When all the votes are counted ... I've won. I'm president! I can throw out the first ball in the little league game.

I look over at Doris. She has a tear in her eye. I go over and give her my last clean tissue. We shake hands.

She opens up her box of doughnuts and offers me one. She really has class. I want her in my cabinet, or even better—I'll make her my first lady!